BIRD-BONKERS STANLEY

BY GRIFF

Hyperion Books for Children
New York

. . . for mum & dad X! X!

Text and illustrations © 2001 by Andrew Griffin
The author would like to thank Barbara Taylor for her bird knowledge.

Printed in Hong Kong
ISBN 0-7868-0683-4
First published in Great Britain in 2001 by *ticktock* Publishing Ltd.,
First U.S. edition, 2001
1 3 5 7 9 10 8 6 4 2
Library of Congress Cataloging-in-Publication Data on file.

Visit www.hyperionchildrensbooks.com

Anyone who knows Stanley
knows that he is not what you'd call "cool."
Today, however, he *is* cold. . . .

In fact,
he's absolutely *freezing*!

When it's this cold, Stanley wishes he could keep warm, like other animals.

He would be warmer if he had . . .

. . . **fatty blubber,** like a whale,

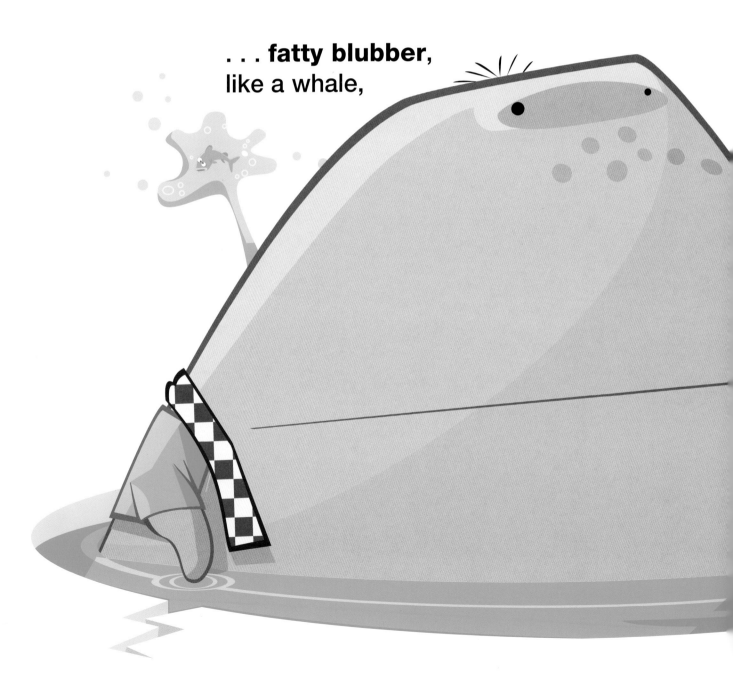

. . . **thick fur**,
like a polar bear,

. . . or **lots of hair**,
like a mountain goat.

Better still,
if he had **feathers!**

With feathers, he could do what birds do and fly somewhere warm.

But not all birds fly
away for the winter.

This is Gordon.

Gordon is a pigeon who lives near Stanley, and he never goes *anywhere*.

He may be sitting on top of the garden shed,

eating in the
vegetable patch,

or drinking in
the fountain.

Stanley knows a lot about pigeons.

Pigeons talk to each other in pigeon English, which sounds a little like this . . . "COO COO COO"

Some people say pigeons are dirty, but a good shake helps rid them of bugs, lice, ticks, and fleas. Then they give themselves a dusting-down with powder produced from the ends of their feathers.

Like other birds, pigeons are covered with feathers, which keep them warm and help them to fly.

After playing in puddles, you usually need a bath, but birds use puddles as a bath. They wash in the rainwater and use their beaks to comb themselves.

Don't try this at home!

Pigeons used to be cliff dwellers and still like to build their untidy nests on ledges.

But as interesting as Gordon is, he'd never be able to take Stanley to a sunnier place. For that, Stanley would need a bigger bird . . .

. . .one as **BIG** and *strong* as an ostrich!

Ostriches have huge legs
and are very good runners.

But they are *so*
heavy they can't fly!

Penguins wouldn't mind
the vacation, but they can't fly either!

Hummingbirds fly very well and very fast . . .

but they never visit Stanley's garden.

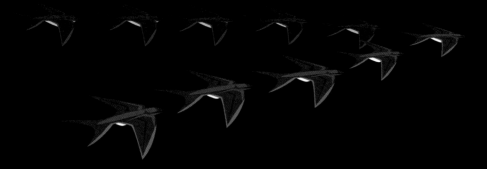

Swallows do, and they
always go away for the winter.

But they fly huge distances every day
without even stopping for a sandwich!

Stanley knows that birds come in all shapes and sizes.

Peacocks are huge show-offs and never go out without dressing up!

Pelicans can keep food in their big, baggy bills. (Bill is also short for William, which is a pelican's middle name.)

↑ (kiwi bird)

Kiwis are ugly on the outside but sweet on the inside.

← (kiwi fruit)   And neither can fly!

Parrots are often very brightly colored. They are also good at copying people's voices—so watch what you say!

Birds of Prey

BIRDS
b
c
d
e
f
g
h
i
j
k
l
m
n
o
p

Maybe Stanley needs a bird of prey! They are big and strong, great fliers, and **love** their food. Not only that…

But owls only come out at night.

Stanley wouldn't be able to see where they were going!

Maybe a vulture would be better?

**Vultures come out
during the day . . .**

but tend to fly in circles
for *hours* waiting for food.

That's no use
to Stanley!

How about
a falcon?

Falcons are **very** fast fliers . . .

but they are far too small to carry Stanley!

How about an eagle?

Eagles are **HUGE** and can carry an animal as big as a sheep!

But an eagle only picks up a sheep to eat it, or feed it to her chicks!

Stanley changes his mind. . . .

Who needs another bird when you can look after a pigeon like Gordon?

And besides . . .

. . . you don't need feathers to fly.

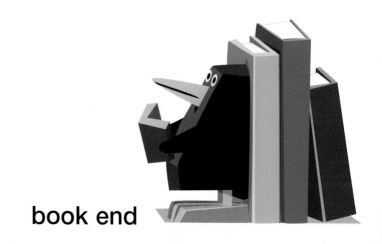

book end